For Al, my pal – love, Niki

Clarion Books · a Houghton Mifflin Company imprint · 215 Park Avenue South, New York, NY 10003 · Copyright © 2006 by Niki Daly
The illustrations were executed in watercolor, pen, and digital media. · The text was set in 19-point Myriad Tilt.
All rights reserved. · For information about permission to reproduce selections from this book, write to Permissions,
Houghton Mifflin Company, 215 Park Avenue South, New York, NY 10003. · www.houghtonmifflinbooks.com · Printed in China
Library of Congress Cataloging-in-Publication Data · Daly, Niki. · Welcome to Zanzibar Road / Niki Daly.   p. cm.
Summary: After moving into the house on Zanzibar Road that her neighbors helped her build, Mama Jumbo decides to
share it with Little Chico. ISBN 0-618-64926-3 · [1. Elephants—Fiction. 2. Chickens—Fiction. 3. Animals—Fiction.
4. Africa—Fiction.] I. Title. · PZ7.D1715 Wel 2006 · [E]—dc22 · 2005021758
ISBN-13: 978-0-618-64926-6 · ISBN-10: 0-618-64926-3
SCP 10 9 8 7 6 5 4 3 2 1

Welcome to Zanzibar Road

Story and Pictures by Niki Daly

Clarion Books · New York

CONTENTS

CHAPTER ONE
Mama Jumbo Builds a House 2

CHAPTER TWO
Something Is Missing 7

CHAPTER THREE
Where's Little Chico? 12

CHAPTER FOUR
A Shadow on the Wall 19

CHAPTER FIVE
A Party on Zanzibar Road 24

CHAPTER ONE
Mama Jumbo Builds a House

One hot day in Africa, Mama Jumbo
was walking down Zanzibar Road.
"What a nice place to live," she thought.
She counted the houses.
1, 2, 3, 4, 5, 6 ... and a pawpaw tree.

"I do love pawpaws," said Mama Jumbo.

"I think I'll build a house here and settle down."

3

Mama Jumbo found a pile of scrap.
"I can turn this scrap
into a house," she thought.

No sooner had she started to build than
a little monkey named Juju came by.
"May I help?" asked Juju.
"Thank you. That would be very kind,"
said Mama Jumbo.

Bang! Bang! hammered Juju.
When the other neighbors
heard the noise, they asked
if they could help, too.

Soon the house was built. But something was missing.

"I need a number," said Mama Jumbo.
"7-Up!" cried Juju,
finding a rusty old store sign.
Mama Jumbo lifted Juju
so he could hang the number
above her door.

Everyone stood back and admired
Mama Jumbo's new house.

"Thank you all. I think I'm going to be very happy
living at Number 7-Up Zanzibar Road," said Mama Jumbo.

CHAPTER TWO
Something Is Missing

Mama Jumbo was all alone in her house. Something was missing.

"I know," said Mama Jumbo. "I'll see if one of
my new friends would like to share my house."

Mama Jumbo asked Juju
if he would like to live with her.
"No, thank you,"
said Juju.
"I like it up here."

Mama Jumbo asked Buti
if he would like to share her house.
But Buti said that he had
his own house—right on his back!

Baba Jive made too much noise to live with Mama Jumbo.

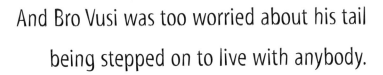

Oh, dear! Nobody wanted to live with Mama Jumbo.

But wait! There was Little Chico. He looked and smelled

as if he needed someone to look after him.

"Can I come live with you?"
asked Little Chico,
following Mama Jumbo.
"Okay," said Mama Jumbo.
"But only if you take a bath
when we get home."
"What's a bath?" asked Little Chico.

Mama Jumbo filled
a cooking pot with water and
added some bubble bath.
"That's a bath," said Mama Jumbo.
"Now, climb in, and
I'll make you nice and clean."

When Little Chico climbed out,
he smelled like strawberry bubblegum.
And while he dried in the sun,
Mama Jumbo sewed a snazzy
pair of pajamas for him.

At bedtime,
Mama Jumbo rocked and
sang a Tula Tula lullaby.
"Good night, my Little Chico,"
whispered Mama Jumbo.
"Good night, Mama,"
said Little Chico sleepily.

Outside, a big melon moon smiled down on them.
Mama Jumbo was happy because her house
was starting to feel like a home.

CHAPTER THREE
Where's Little Chico?

Mama Jumbo woke up feeling very excited.

"What a lovely day for spoiling my Little Chico!"

she thought.

But when she looked for Little Chico,

she could not find him.

She looked inside.

She looked outside.

But Mama Jumbo could not see Little Chico anywhere.
"Oh, dear," she said with a sigh. "Perhaps Little Chico
does not want to live with me anymore.
Or maybe he has gotten lost."

Quickly, she set off down the road to look for him.

She popped into Louie-Louie's Spaza.

But she did not see Little Chico.

She peeped into
Bro Vusi's bookmobile.
But she did not see Little Chico.

She poked her head into
Baba Jive's club.
Little Chico was
nowhere to be seen.

"Oh, Little Chico,"
sighed Mama Jumbo tearfully.
"Where can you be?"

Poor Mama Jumbo walked the town flat,

but still she could not find Little Chico.

"Why are you looking so sad, Mama Jumbo?" asked Juju.

"I've lost Little Chico!

And now my heart is broken," she cried.

"Just wait until I find him.

I'll pull his tail for making me worry so."

Juju laughed. "Oh, Mama Jumbo.
Little Chico is sitting on your head!"
"Little Chico, are you sitting
on my head?" scolded Mama Jumbo.
"Yes, I am," said Little Chico.
"Well, jump down at once!"
said Mama Jumbo.

Mama Jumbo was so pleased
to see her darling
that she did not pull his tail.
Instead, she hugged him.

17

Now the day was done, and Mama Jumbo felt disappointed.

"I wanted so much to spoil you today," she said sadly.

"Oh, Mama, I've had a lovely day!" said Little Chico.

"I've looked under the bed. I've looked on top of the roof.

I've been to Louie-Louie's Spaza, filled with sweeties.

Then I popped into Bro Vusi's mobile library

and saw lots and lots of books.

I heard jazzy music in Baba Jive's club.

And now we are having a corn barbecue

and watching the sun go to bed."

"I'm glad you're happy," said Mama Jumbo.

"But no more sitting on heads!"

CHAPTER FOUR
A Shadow on the Wall

One day, Mama Jumbo put on her

"Go-to-town, knock-'em-down, ding-dong" hat.

Then she and Little Chico went out and

bought a prickly pear tree in a pretty pink clay pot.

"Now, where shall we put it?"

she asked when they got home.

"Here!" cried Little Chico,

pointing to a spot outside his window.

That night, Little Chico woke up with a terrible fright.

A spiky-haired monster was in the room.

"Mama! Mama!" he cried.

Mama Jumbo jumped out of bed.

"What's the matter, my darling?" she asked.

"Look, Mama!" said Little Chico. "A terrible monster!

"Oh, Little Chico. That's not a monster,"
said Mama Jumbo.

"See? It's just the shadow of the prickly pear tree
falling on the wall. Now, go to sleep."

But Little Chico could not go to sleep.
"Mama! Mama! The prickly pear monster
is still looking at me," he whispered.
So Mama Jumbo got out of bed again,
collected some things, and went outside.

Under a bright African moon,
she dressed the prickly pear tree
until it looked like . . .

...a Mama Elephant wearing a
"Go-to-town, knock-'em-down, ding-dong" hat.

Little Chico smiled and waved

to the friendly shadow on the wall.

"Nighty-night, Mama."

"Good night, my darling," Mama Jumbo said,

and she climbed back into bed.

CHAPTER FIVE
A Party on Zanzibar Road

Mama Jumbo was stirring something in a bowl.

"What are you doing?" asked Little Chico.

"I'm making a birthday cake," answered Mama Jumbo.

"Whose birthday is it?" asked Little Chico.

"Yours!" said Mama Jumbo.

"How many candles will I have?" asked Little Chico.

"I think three will be just right," said Mama Jumbo.

She poured the mixture into a cake tin and baked it.

At three o'clock, Mama Jumbo lit the candles.

Little Chico took a deep breath . . .

Knock! Knock! Somebody was at the door.

It was Juju, Buti, and Kwela.

Mama Jumbo invited them in.

"Now you may blow out your candles," said Mama Jumbo.

Again, Little Chico took a deep breath . . .

Knock! Knock! Somebody was at the door.

This time it was Baba Jive, Louie-Louie, and Bro Vusi.

"Come in, we're having a party!" said Mama Jumbo.

They all stood around as Little Chico

took another deep breath . . .

"Knock! Knock!" said Juju.

"Who's there?" they all asked.

"Willy!" said Juju mischievously.

"Willy who?" they all asked.

"Will he or won't he blow out the candles?"
joked Juju.

Everyone laughed. Then Little Chico took a very deep breath . . .

and blew out 1 . . . 2 . . . 3 candles!

"Hip hip hooray!" they cheered.
Then they sang "Happy Birthday"
while Mama Jumbo cut the cake.

Afterward, Baba Jive played his jazzy sax.

Soon the party was cooking with music and laughter.

"You are the sweetest little chicken

in the whole of Africa!"

cried Mama Jumbo as she danced with Little Chico.

"And you're the hottest mama

in the whole wide world!"

said Little Chico.

Then they all danced the Funky Chicken

until the pawpaws rocked in the pawpaw tree

outside Number 7-Up Zanzibar Road.

Louie~Louie

MamaJumbo

Little Chico

BroVusi

Kwela